The Structure

The Structure

Book 3 Life on Delta Psi

Jerry Cook

Tiffany Cook

Storytelling Jerry

CONTENTS

The man-made light, lit up the sky, keeping the weather a temperate 73 degrees Fahrenheit. Without worry of inclement weather, the people of Delta Psi could live peacefully. Although they had for the last 245 years on The Structure, Delta Psi, they were the last humans of Earth and had kept their population to a minimum based on IQ levels. Those struggling to "survive" would be culled during their teen life, during their "survival test" where the students are taken to a remote location on Delta Psi to test their skills of survival but only if they're failing their classes. Each year, the death count rises by at least a student, or falls by two, but never is there no student who dies during the survival test. The chance to "Pass" that year is allowed if they survive, though it will only happen again the following year, if they aren't passing their class. Schooling in 2275 isn't like the times of school on Earth, as High School classes have become, one. One A.I. controlled cyborg per classroom that can instruct each student exceptionally, and it's up to the student to accept their learning regime. The A.I Teacher Mr. Clark has a face that looks a lot like the face of the 2013 retro film of superman. A gimmick that their predecessors felt would make a resounding presence for the children as they learned. Though, it was recycled and used for every one of the male teachers and the students found it redundant to their learning. The only survivors from Earth had been the rich and the famous, or more so their offspring.

Most notable of those families was that of our friend, Jack. As it just so happened, his ancestor was the creator of Delta Psi.

We continue our story following Jack, Mikhael and now, Sarah, as they gather up new Survivalnauts and attempt to survive the coming test.

The students were gathering at the front gate as a cloud began to form in the skies of Delta Psi. Most noticed the cloud and were drawn to it, almost as bugs to a light, unknowingly seeking the abyss, while the students prepared for their day, and the struggles that were ahead.

Survival-nots?

[6:45] Click.

The clicking drove Jack to put his digital watch into his backpack.

"What do you mean, I up and left you?" Mikhael asked "Are you trying to say I died? Ha, HA don't make me laugh so hard, Jack!"

"Well, you did!" Jack started to walk faster. "Come on, we're going to be late."

Mikhael quickly followed behind, inquiring more about the dreams, to which Jack began explaining the events that took place. The boys were almost too school when they were passed by the star bus. The star bus brought some of the kids to school who lived out near the Plateau, since the distance was deemed too far for them to walk to school safely.

"Hosiah, rides the star bus every morning." Mikhael pointed out as it passed. "You think that's why we never really talked?"

"Well, we definitely have a reason to talk now." Jack rounded the corner at their high school, Delta Psi High. "We've got a survival test ahead of us."

"Hey Jack, Mikhael!" "How are ya?" A familiar voice called out to the boys.

"Sarah?" Jack was confused. "Why are you talking to us?"

"Are you just going to make fun of us?"

Sarah cackled. "You dweebs!"

"I've got to take the test too." "Everyone with failing grades has to take the test, you dweebs should know that."

Sarah was one of the more popular kids amongst their class, being one of the Founders granddaughters landed her the spotlight in his youth. The spotlight, however, did not help her studies.

Jack and Mikhael gave one another a quick glance and in unison asked her "Will you join our tribe?!"

Sarah gave the boys a smile. "I thought you'd be too scared to ask me, of course I'll join you!"

[0715] Click.

"We should try to recruit some others to our tribe anyway, Jack." "We don't want to be outnumbered if some of the worst kids make a tribe." Mikhael glances at the group of children waiting to get into the detention room.

Jack stepped past the gate. "Well, we won't make any new tribe members just standing around!"

The three, unlikely to have befriended one another any other time, had just set themselves on gaining more tribe mates. With Sarah at the helm, their chances would be higher, as she's one of the more popular students in the school, all the children look up to her. Even though her grades in class are failing, she is still the star pupil of the school, and most people would love to be her friend, still. The life of all the failing students was about to change, be it for worse, or better. As Jack made his way into the school yard, he noticed Hosiah was watching him. Without skipping a beat, he spun on his heels and asked the boy "Hosiah, will you join our tribe?"

Hosiah returned with his own question. "What's the name again? Survival-nots? Don't that mean we ain't gonna survive?"

Jack chortled "Survival-nauts. Those navigating the skills of survival! So, are you in?"

The other students around them heard their conversation and a few of them laughed, though, a few more stepped forward to join them. With Jack, Mikhael, Sarah and Hosiah, their chances were even higher but with the addition of Alex and Milo and Meelo, the twins, their tribe was looking like an actual tribe. Milo and Meelo were failing their class as well, although their parents are well known scientists. The two had always felt as though they were just a hindrance to the rest of Delta Psi. Whereas Alex had spent his whole life in luxury. Living in the high rise in the uptown area of town, Miniora, Alex was able to make to so far in school because of his family's status. The boy had been failing throughout his years and continuing through the grades because his family had pull with the council. His thought was that they were trying to get rid of him. Using the survival test as a means to remove him from their life, so they can start over with their new child, his brother, Al-ecks. His family being one of the richest families of old Earth, their pull on Delta Psi continued.

As they all made their way onto the school grounds, Jack brought up his dreams from the night before. Reflecting on the deaths of his classmates and explaining to them what had happened, Jack made it clear that he felt that all those things could happen again, starting today. If the children were to survive, they would have to band together, and fight. Though, they did not know for sure what it was they would be fighting. At this point in time, the children could only imagine the monstrosity that could be "Krollo" as Jack says they are.

"A fish like man being. I don't know exactly how to explain his looks! Alien?" Jack continued "The real worry, I think, is the crazy hybrids I saw in my dream. The Alpha really had it out for me."

[0735] Click-zzt. The clock brought attention to itself with the noise.

"It's 7:35. We had better get to our classroom. Anyone else who wants to join, we'll pick them up on the star bus."

The group of teenagers agreed, and though a couple of them had a different classroom, they all set off to their classes, in preparation for their day. Afraid of what may happen to them as the dark cloud began to cover the sky.

[0745] School bells begin ringing to signal that class is going to start soon.

Jack pulled out his chair and sat down, throwing his backpack on his desk so he could look through it one more time before they set out on their adventure. As he was digging through his backpack, he found an odd, shaped piece of wood at the bottom of his pack, as though long forgotten by him, it had been floating around the bottom of his backpack for a while, it looked. Shaped like a strange triangle, the odd piece of geometry seemed to sing to Jack, almost humming. As Jack began to get lost in thought while staring into his little piece of art, the teacher, Mr. Clark, began to get himself set up at the front of the class. His A.I.

processors whirring and clicking like an old model desktop computer, super retro. Time seemed to almost stand still and things around him fell silent as Jack got lost staring at this odd, shaped piece of wood. He began to feel uneasy just as Mikhael broke the silence.

"What the heck is that?"

Jack jumped, startled by the question. "What is what? This?" he held up the oddity.

"I don't know, but I have a feeling we'll find out. It's humming to me."

The two boys focused extremely closely on the triangular wood and listened for the humming.

Ten seconds.

Twenty seconds. Thirty seconds.

After what felt like forever, the clock on the wall changed to [0800] and the bell sounded once more, to inform the students that class had begun. This startled both Mikhael and Jack, and he dropped the piece of wood back into his backpack. Mr. Clark began his daily greetings to the class, offering each student a good morning and welcome to class, before beginning his speech about the survival test.

Mostly the boring stuff, according to Sarah.

When he was done saying good morning, he began his announcement.

Today marks the two hundred and twenty third annual Delta Psi High survival test. I hope all of you got your sleep and ate your Wheatie-o's this morning, because it's about to be a bumpy ride. All the failing students will be placed onto a star bus and taken to a point in the Great Stone Mountains, where you'll have to fight, or band together, to survive the harsh environment. You will have three days to make it from your drop off point to the rendezvous point, where you'll be picked up, by me, or another teacher and a star bus. If you pass this test, you'll all go on to the next grade, but if you pass the test and then continue to fail next year, you'll just be brought right back here again for the two hundred and twenty fourth annual survival test, next year. We leave for the Great Stone Mountains at 0830. Any questions?

The students all looked around the room and realized a few of them weren't there. Jesse was the first to mention it. "Where are the other students?" Though some of the smarter kids knew that they didn't need to be there. All the kids whose grades were a 3.2 or higher got the day off from school and some were even afforded vacations until school would return in 4 months. The extra time was given to allow for any mourning of their peers that needed to be done. This wasn't the case with this class, as most of them were enemies. Jesse and Bart, short for Bartholomew, were the bullies of the school. Being seniors who'd been held back twice, the two were 6-year survivors of the culling of the test. It's because of this fact that most of the students felt like they were staying on purpose. Jesse's home life wasn't the best, as his mother and father were cryogenically frozen in the year 2042 and still remembered much of life on Earth. Being unable to adjust to their new life on Delta Psi, they were taken over with depression and addiction for hallucinogenic drugs. Because of this, they overdosed on the medication 5 years ago and Jesse has since moved in with Bart and his family. The two acted as brothers, though at home Jesse was treated like the golden child, so to speak, while Bart was constantly criticized for his actions. Bartholomew had grown up like most rich children, a golden spoon in his hand and a golden bowl of ice cream in the other. His parents always gave him what he wanted until Jesse moved in with them. Because the boys were friends though, they couldn't bring themselves to fight one another. So, they took out their frustrations on the other students. The council of Delta Psi High had seen this and chose to allow the students to stay in the school, to perhaps graduate with honors, or so they say.

Mr. Clark smiled at Jesse "Well, they're on vacation of course." The answer, none too wrong, yet none too right, as life outside of the school was experiencing its first storm. The thunder boomed and the lightning cracked across the sky, causing the students to jump.

[0815] Clickzzt.

The sound, like an echo within Jack's ear. Ever so faintly he could hear the clicking of the electronics inside the clock. His mind unable to think of anything else besides the time, and their survival. With his new entourage, or tribe as they were calling themselves, the Survivalnauts, Mikhael, Sarah, Alex, and the twins, he felt like his chances were even better. In his dreams, Jack could recall that only Hosiah and Mikhael joined up with him, but both fell prey to the survival test. His plan this time would be to keep as many of them alive as possible, including their parents. Jack turned to Mikhael and began to explain his plan.

I think when we land, we will head to our old camp spot. You know, the one where my parents used to take us? We'll get down there and set up camp, since we only have 3 days. It's only about a day and a half hike from there to the rendezvous point, and I want to be there first. We have to meet with Krollo, at least I think that's what his name was.

Mikhael just nodded in agreement, like a bobblehead. Jack couldn't tell whether or not to trust that he knew the plan, but he had to have faith in his friend.

Mr. Clark stood up in front of the class just as the clock changed.

[0825] Clickzt

Alright class, we're going to line up along the south wall of the classroom and then single file we'll walk down to the star bus loading bay.

The students all hurriedly got up and ran to the wall, hoping to be able to stand in line next to their friends or tribe members for the test, Jesse and Burt included. As they made their way to the loading area, Jack asked some of the other students if they would join his tribe, to no avail. The same went for Mikhael, as both the boys happened to be unpopular among the other students. As they shuffled slowly onto the star bus, Jack could see the other students all loading onto the other buses, and he noticed the entire senior class was loading as well. The clouds in the sky causing a slight panic among the students as they'd never seen a dark cloud before made it even more interesting to Jack that so many students were taking the test. To Jack, the situation felt like it was staged. A set up, to goad the students into a panic so they won't work together. As he shuffled down the corridor to his seat, he thought about his dreams, and if Krollo had made his landing at the rendezvous yet.

"Alone, you're not."

Krollos voice came to mind as he thought about what may happen. Given his larger tribe, Jack felt that their chances were much better now. Gazing out at the rolling landscape, Jack's thoughts turned to his dreams of Krollo. He recalled those enigmatic visions that had spurred him to rally his friends. In those dreams, Krollo stood as a beacon of guidance, a mentor of sorts. Jack envisioned a figure cloaked in shadows, whispering cryptic messages that seemed to hold the key to their survival.

As the star bus traversed the rugged terrain, the vibrations beneath Jack's feet seemed to echo the uncertainty he felt. He glanced at Mikhael, who was lost in his own thoughts, his brow furrowed with a mixture of determination and concern. Mikhael's unwavering loyalty had been the bedrock upon which their tribe was built.

Jack leaned back in his seat; his gaze fixed on the horizon. The storm outside mirrored the tempestuous journey that lay ahead. He thought of his parents, a surge of determination coursing through him. He had to succeed in this test, not only for his own sake but for the Survival-nauts, for Mikhael, for Sarah, for Alex, and for the twins.

Amid the rhythmic hum of the star bus, Jack's thoughts wove a tapestry of hopes and uncertainties. The great stone mountains loomed closer; their imposing silhouettes etched against the turbulent sky. As the vehicle pressed on, the dream of meeting Krollo merged with the reality of their imminent challenge. The storm outside raged on, a testament to the trials that awaited them.

With each passing mile, Jack's resolve grew stronger. He was determined to lead his newfound tribe through this trial, to safeguard their unity, and to unlock the mysteries of Krollo's guidance to find the light. The star bus pressed forward, carrying the Survival-nauts towards the heart of the mountains and the destiny that awaits them.

2 |

The Arrival.

Upon arriving at the base of the great stone mountains, the star bus came to a smooth halt. The doors slid open with a soft hiss, and a gust of cool, mountain air swept through the interior. The storm that had accompanied them on their journey had dissipated, leaving behind a serene landscape bathed in the soft light of the setting sun. As Jack and his fellow Survivalnauts disembarked, they admired the majestic peaks that surrounded them. The mountains seemed to reach for the heavens, their rugged surfaces bearing the scars of time. The air was crisp and invigorating, carrying with it a sense of adventure and challenge. With a quick glance at Mikhael, Jack could sense the mixture of determination and curiosity that mirrored his own feelings. The twins chattered excitedly; their youthful energy undimmed by the trials ahead. Sarah's steady gaze revealed a calm resolve, while Alex's infectious enthusiasm was palpable.

"We're here" Jack murmured, a mixture of excitement and trepidation in his voice.

The Great Stone Mountain loomed majestically before them, a natural wonder that held an air of ancient grandeur. Its rugged peaks kissed the sky, their imposing presence a testament to the passage of time. As Jack and his companions stood at its base, a sense of awe washed over them, their gazes drawn upwards to the monumental visages carved into the rock face. The setting sun's gentle glow bathed the scene in pink and blue light, casting elongated shadows that seemed to breathe life into the stone. The Great Stone Mountain's surface was etched with intricate patterns, the result of millennia of weathering and erosion. Its towering silhouette was framed by a star-studded sky, each celestial light a witness to the history and stories that had unfolded here. Four colossal figures gazed solemnly from the mountainside. Their profiles hewn with remarkable precision. The natural contours of the rock had been transformed into the dignified visages of past leaders, their expressions a mixture of wisdom, determination, and

timelessness. Each carving was a tribute to the leaders who had shaped the destiny of the land, a

reminder of the enduring ideals they represented. The sunlight revealed the delicate details etched into the stone. The chiseled features bore the weight of history, lines and creases etched into the stone like

chapters in a story. The eyes of the figures seemed to hold a silent watch over the landscape, their gaze reaching far beyond the horizon.

As a crisp breeze swept through the mountain's craggy terrain, it seemed to carry with it whispers of

history and the tales of those who had passed through this place. The Great Stone Mountain stood as a

monument to the resilience of nature and the legacy of humanity's endeavors, a place where the forces

of nature and human artistry converged. Jack and his friends stood in reverent silence, their thoughts a mixture of wonder and reflection. The Great Stone Mountain held a quiet power, a blend of natural beauty and the indomitable spirit of those who had carved their mark into its stone. As they gazed upon

this majestic tableau, they felt a connection to the past and a sense of determination to forge their own destinies in the face of the challenges that awaited them on this path of survival and discovery.

With the Great Stone Mountain as their backdrop and the moon as their guiding light, Jack and his companions set to work preparing for their first night in the rugged terrain. The wind whispered through the craggy landscape, and the air held a chill that hinted at the challenges of the night ahead. Their survival instincts kicked in, and they wasted no time in securing their camp. The Survivalnauts scoured the area for suitable spots to set up their campsite. They found a sheltered enclave nestled between rock formations. Using the resources they had brought and the natural materials around them, they

constructed a makeshift shelter using sturdy branches, large leaves, and their survival gear. The shelter

would provide some protection from the elements and the cool night air. Jack and Mikhael gathered dry twigs, leaves, and small branches for a campfire. Fire was essential not only for warmth but also for cooking and boosting morale. With careful arrangement, they managed to ignite a fire using a flint and steel from their multi-tool. The crackling flames cast flickering shadows against the stone walls, creating an atmosphere of camaraderie for the teens. The twins searched for berries, while Hosiah fashioned a fishing pole and caught some fish. The group shared their provisions, and they used their portable water filters to collect and purify water from a nearby stream. It was a simple meal, but it provided the

sustenance they needed for the night ahead. Safety was paramount, and the Survivalnauts decided to

take shifts for keeping watch throughout the night. Sarah and Alex took the first shift, followed by the twins, and finally Jack and Mikhael. Each shift involved scanning the surroundings for any signs of danger and tending to the fire to ensure its constant presence. Their first night seemed to go off without a hitch,

until Jack noticed the sky begin to light up, just as it did in his dream.

As the light began to paint the sky with shades of gold and green, casting a warm glow across the rugged landscape of the Great Stone Mountain, the Survivalnauts were stirred from their makeshift campsite. They emerged from their shelter, stretching and yawning, ready to face the challenges.

Unbeknownst to them, as the light began to illuminate the horizon, another group had been watching from the shadows. Jesse and Bart, two figures driven by their own motives, had been observing the Survivalnauts from a distance. Their eyes gleamed with a mix of curiosity and a hint of mischief as they plotted their next move.

As the light of dawn revealed the campsite, Jesse and Bart seized their opportunity. They approached the campsite with stealth, their footsteps muffled by the uneven terrain. The Survivalnauts were focused on their morning tasks—packing up their gear, stoking the remnants of last night's campfire, and discussing the plans for the day.

The first sign of trouble came when a rustling in the nearby bushes caught Jack's attention. He turned to look, his instincts on high alert. Before he could react, Jesse and Bart sprang from their hiding places, their faces obscured by masks. The suddenness of the ambush left the Survivalnauts momentarily stunned, their hands instinctively reaching for their multi-tools.

"Who are you? What do you want?" Mikhael's voice held a mixture of caution and challenge as he confronted the intruders.

Jesse and Bart exchanged glances, their lips curling into smirks. "Just a little test, Survivalnauts," Jesse replied cryptically. "We want to see how well you handle unexpected situations."

Sarah's brow furrowed with suspicion. "Why would you do this?"

Bart's chuckle was mirthless. "Think of it as a trial by fire. We've been watching you, and we think you might have what it takes."

Tension hung in the air as the two groups faced off. The light continued its glow, casting long shadows across the scene. The Survivalnauts exchanged wary glances, their minds racing to process the situation.

Jack stepped forward, his gaze steady. "If it's a challenge you want, then challenge us fair and square. No ambushes, no masks. Let's settle this with respect."

Jesse and Bart regarded him for a moment before exchanging another glance. Slowly, they removed their masks, revealing faces that bore a mixture of determination and curiosity.

"Fair enough," Jesse said, a hint of admiration in his voice. "We were just doing what the council asked us to do, anyway."

Bart quickly jabbed him in the ribs, "We weren't supposed to say anything about that!" The boys quickly began to bicker amongst themselves. "Stop!" Sarah yelled out as she stepped over to the two boys. "What the heck is going on here? Did you just say, what the council asked you to do?"

The group of kids all settled for a moment to pay attention. "Explain yourselves." Jack insisted as he held his spear up to Jesse and Bart. "I will use this on you, if I have too." The boy quickly gave one another a glance and with a gulp, Jesse began his story.

Well, we were doing pretty bad in our classes and Mr. Clark told us he had a special assignment for us. So, we took him up on the offer and listened to what he had to say. Of course, all he said was to go see the council.

Bart began with his part as well,
Then the council was acting real strange, right. They kept asking us if we were sure we could complete our task. Pshh. They should have known I'm a failure.

Jesse continued,
So, then they started asking us if we'd ever killed before. Well, we haven't really. We said we did so they'd get on with it, though. We told them that in previous survival tests we'd killed the other participants to pass. It was a lie but look! Now, we're here with you! We can like, team up or something.

Jack tossed the idea around in his head and quickly turned to ask his tribe members their opinion, Mikhael was first to detest. "They just told us they were supposed to kill us, Jack!" Sarah quickly agreed, "He's right, they did literally just say that." The twins both gave a shrug and a quick, "Don't ask us!" As they covered their faces. Jack turned back to Jesse and Bart with a puzzled look on his face. "Well, my friends don't want you to join us." Suddenly, the green light from his dreams beamed across the sky. The illumination showed the small cameras within Jesse's eyes as it lit up the sky for five seconds. Alex began pointing at Jesse, "Hey, your eyes are like Mr. Clark's!"

A silence fell over the surroundings as the light faded from the sky. Bart slowly stepped over next to Jack, "I'm just going to step right over here, okay?" His voice wavered as he moved. Jesse slowly stood straight upright, unhuman entirely. "The light will guide you, Jack." The last of his humanity suddenly leaving his face as the A.I. took over. "I am J-3-5-5-3. Code: Jesse. Survival test mission: Failure, redirecting path to new directive." His body suddenly lunged at Jack, reaching for his neck. "Must eliminate, targets." Bart started screaming as he picked up the spear that Jack had dropped and began sticking it in Jesse's ribs. The stabbing had no effect, as not even a drop of blood came from the wound. Hosiah and Mikhael quickly joined in the fray, grabbing ahold of Jesse's arms, and pulling them to stop him from choking Jack.

"J-4-C-K, accept your directive." Jesse began to repeat the phrase as Bart shoved the spear deep into his spinal cord and began tearing upward. His voice suddenly slowed as Bart ripped some wiring from the nape of his neck. "J...4...C...K..." His hands loosened around Jack's neck, and he finally pried his neck free. "Holy crap, I almost died!" Jack fell back over a log that was near him and lay flat on the ground as the color quickly returned to his face. "What the heck was that!?" Hosiah jumped and shouted as he waved his arms about. The group all took a moment to gather their thoughts and quickly regrouped, Bart now included. "What did he mean by accept your directive, Jack?" Mikhael asked with a puzzled look on his face. "You're not one of them, are you?" The group turned its full attention to Jack. "No, I don't even know what the heck happened to Jesse. This whole thing does not make sense..." Sarah examined their campsite, "Well, should we bury him?" Alex stopped her, "No, we shouldn't bury him. We should get out of here!" The rest of the group silently agreed with him. Milo and Meelo glanced at one another, as if to keep their words to themselves but Milo quickly spoke up. "We think we should go to the rendezvous point as quickly as possible." Jack stood himself over the robotic corpse of Jesse, "Well, we can't go in the night. We should wait till morning. Plus, the others will have set up camp for the night, as well." He scratched his head in confusion, "But, I don't see why things are so different?" Mikhael noticed the confusion on Jack's face. "What is it, Jack?" He asked, hesitant to know the answer.

"Well, I don't quite understand why things are so different?" He rubbed his head and took a seat on the log he had earlier tripped on. "In my dream; the first night, you, me and Hosiah were together, but we were the only ones. And then the first night, we lost Hosiah in the middle of the night. This time, we've been attacked by some robotic Jesse and Bart. I don't understand why things are so different. I thought that if we prepared and there were more of us, then something like this wouldn't happen." The group gathered around the body of the robotic copy of their classmate. "Well, should we dispose of this?" Bart winced as he lifted the arm. "It still feels like him. That's strange, isn't it?" The group all reached down simultaneously, "Yeah, that is weird. They must have made an exact copy of his looks." Mikhael said as he touched his arm. The others quickly recoiled as their minds began to wander, *What if it's actually, him?*

The thoughts began to freak the kids out, so they quickly picked up the robot and set it in the nearby stream, just big enough for a canoe. The buoyancy of the human-like form kept it afloat as it was sent downstream, far away from their camp. The group quickly regrouped at their camp to sleep and prepare for their trek the next day. After preparing Bart his own place to sleep, they all laid down for the night. As his eyes slowly became heavy, Jack began to think of what may come, and what had happened in his dreams. Their fire began to flicker as Jack closed his eyes, unprepared for what the light may bring.

3

The Wakening.

A strange humming fell on Jack's ears, rhythmic in tone. A voice silently rose in the faintness of his mind, "Jack, you have to use the key." Soft, like his mothers. "Jack, find the answers. You are the only hope..." The voice slowly faded away as his vision seemed to clear up. The large buildings of Delta Psi surrounded him, much like his dreams from the night before. *Okay, now this is getting out of hand...* The words came out, but Jack noticed he hadn't opened his mouth. *Whoa, now that is new!* The sounds of people running and screaming suddenly came from the middle of what looked like downtown, followed by the sound of a large creature, roaring and thrashing about.

Well, that can't be good.

Jack began to walk towards the sounds, almost against his will. His heart pounding as the screams and roars continued, growing louder as he neared the corner of the street. As his foot touched the concrete near the corner, suddenly the world around Jack began to shift, contorting itself into a new image. A large pyramid, surrounded by palm trees. The image began to shift again to another image with even more of these pyramids, surrounded by a dense forest on a tropical planet. The voice returned, *"Will you save them, Jack?"* The strange green light beamed across the sky in the image, tearing through it like a knife to a hunk of butter. *"If you don't, the light will."*

His eyes shot open as the light beamed across the image again, startling him from his sleep. Jack looked around at his friends, *"All asleep I see."* He mumbled to himself as he rolled over. As he turned himself over, Jack caught a shimmer in the night sky, something unusual on Delta Psi. The moon and stars were all fabricated light fixtures that would move as the night progressed, "There shouldn't be any other lights in the sky." He whispered softly. His heart began to race as the shimmer began to move, quickly dropping down somewhere near the rendezvous point. *And that must be Krollo.* His thoughts began to wonder, "But what was that noise in the dream? Was it the hybrids?" He shuddered at the thought. "That would be terrible news." After a few moments there was a loud banging noise, followed by a crackling, like that of one thousand firecrackers going off at once. The light pierced the sky with its green glow, causing Jack to close his eyes. "Holy smokes is that bright!" He lifted his arm to cover his eyes. After five seconds the brightness subsided and Jack was left in silence, surrounded by his friend's quiet snores. He slowly moved his arm away from his face to see if the light had gone when he noticed the shimmer in the distance. It suddenly lifted itself straight up and returned on its path it had come from. "Well, that was odd." He thought to himself as he tried to get comfortable on his makeshift bed. "Maybe it wasn't Krollo?" He turned himself over again, like a rotisserie chicken. "The sun will be up soon; I should get some more sleep." he told himself as he slowly drifted off.

The sun was slowly rising when Hosiah opened his eyes. The others were still asleep, so he got up quietly and grabbed his fishing things. "I'll go catch some fish while they're all asleep, I bet I can catch all kinds of fish up here." His excitement caused him to leave his multi tool behind as he shuffled off to the stream, hoping to get back before the others would wake. "I could come back and make them all breakfast, yeah, that'll get them motivated!" He double checked his knot on his hook and quickly cast into the stream, waiting for a bite. A few moments went by, and he felt a tug on his line, "A fish!" He shouted as he snapped the pole back, pulling the fish out of the water. The small blue gill flopped around on the shore nearby for a second before Hosiah removed the hook. "You're kind of small little guy, but we're hungry. Looks like I'm going to have to keep you anyways, sorry!" He smiled as he tied the fish to a makeshift stringer. "One down, only fifteen more just like that and I could probably feed myself!" He laughed as he cast again. Looming in the distance, a set of eyes had been watching Hosiah from the time he'd left the camp. The usual alpha predator in the mountains, a mountain lion had been following him. It watched in curiosity as he pulled in fish after fish, its tail dancing back and forth in enjoyment. After thirty long minutes, the lion decided it was time to make his move. He slowly approached Hosiah from the rear, silently stepping over tree branches. As it got within thirty feet of the boy, it stopped. Another presence was fast approaching, and the lion could not react, it was struck by the Alpha. Quickly, it was removed from the scene; as if the alpha had been an eraser and the lion, a pencil mark. Hosiah continued to pull more fish from the stream, his count now to seven. Completely unaware of the terrible things that had been happening behind him, he pulled another fish from the stream. A loud screaming came from behind him, like someone was killing a woman, or strangling her to be precise. The wails sent a shiver up his spine, and he quickly gathered his fish and ran back to the camp, still unaware of the presence of the alpha. As he approached the camp, Hosiah felt himself being watched. "Who… Who's there?" He stammered as he asked, afraid of the answer he may receive. "I've got a weapon!" He shouted, as he held up his pouch that he usually carried his multi tool in. "I will use it, if I have too!" He shouted again, as he began to panic and spin around with the noises of movement in the brush. With swiftness, he was gone. The alpha attacked him, quickly engulfing him in one bite as his fishing pole and stringer of fish fell to the ground, his hand still gripping it tightly.

Jack sat upright, as if he had been awake the whole time. "Well, did everyone sleep okay? Because I sure didn't." He laughed to himself as he stood up. Sarah quickly noticed that Hosiah was missing, "Hosiah isn't in the camp!" She shouted as she pointed to his makeshift bed. Mikhael and the others quickly got up from their slumber and began to call out for Hosiah, hoping he would answer back. "We've got to find him." Jack looked around at the group all searching the same places, "Perhaps, we could spread out and search near the camp?" Jacks voice shook from the thoughts of his dream. "He's got to be around here somewhere." The group set off in pairs to find their tribe mate, Jack and Mikhael, Meelo and Milo, Alex and Sarah and Bart followed so he wasn't alone. They each took turns directing one another on where to look next, when Bart pointed out the smell of fish nearby. "That's got to be him!" Jack became excited at the thought that nothing had happened to Hosiah, only to be let down as he climbed over a large rock to find his friend's hand still holding the pole. The gruesome sight caused Jack to vomit uncontrollably. The others' curiosity piqued as Jack began to projectile vomit, they each took their turn peaking over the rocks. Each one sickened by the sight they had seen, they puked together. Bart gathered himself for a moment, "You know; in a way, this is bonding." His joke didn't sit well, even with himself as he continued to puke. After five long minutes of vomiting, Jack noticed the prints in the dirt seemed to look like clawed flippers. A shiver went up his spine at the thought of the Alpha. In his dreams, the alpha was a large shark-like alien hybrid. It could even speak in languages other than its own. A terribly remarkable sight, even in a dream.

The kids soon gathered themselves and returned to their camp, distraught over the death of their friend. "We have to leave; we need to get to the rendezvous!" Milo began to panic, his life flashing before his eyes as he thought of his death. "I don't want to die out here!" Meelo began crying out as well. Jack began packing his things while the others all gathered and cried together. "You know, we will die if we stay here." His words fell on them like a hammer, "Okay, Jack. We're going." Sarah reluctantly began picking up her things. The others joined in packing their things, soon after. Jack began formulating his plan, "We'll hike down the mountain, along the river. It's the closest path to the rendezvous; and there's fresh water and food. It's about a two-day hike; but we've managed to make it at least part of the way, our first day." Mikhael tossed his pack over his shoulder, "Well, shouldn't we be off?" Jack laughed, "Great enthusiasm." Sarah chortled, "So, just down the hill we go? Like all of this didn't just happen?"

Jack turned to her, "Yes, Sarah. We can't let this stop us from reaching our goal. We must *survive*."

The Survival-nauts descended the towering stone mountain with a cautious determination, their every step echoing against the rugged terrain. The air was thick with the scent of ancient rocks and the distant rumble of the river below. The path carved into the mountain's side revealed a breathtaking panorama of sheer cliffsides and towering trees that stood sentinel over the winding river. As they made their way down, the rock cliffsides provided both perilous drops and awe-inspiring views. Large trees, their roots intertwining with the rock, leaned out precariously over the river, their branches offering patches of shade and mystery. The Survival-nauts navigated this natural obstacle course with a blend of skill and anticipation, mindful of the unpredictable challenges nature could throw their way. The river, a ribbon of liquid silver, meandered through the valley below, carrying whispers of secrets as it flowed. The rhythmic rush of water blended with the occasional creaking of ancient branches, creating a symphony of nature that accompanied the Survival-nauts on their descent. As the group moved further downstream, a sudden hush fell over the environment. The wind whispered through the leaves, and the rustle of the river seemed to soften. The Survival-nauts exchanged wary glances, sensing a change in the atmosphere. It was then that they felt the ground vibrate beneath their feet, a low-frequency resonance that seemed to emanate from the very heart of the forest.

Unexpectedly, the Alpha made its presence known. A creature of alien design, it emerged from the depths of the river, a hybrid of shark and otherworldly elements. Its scales shimmered with an otherworldly iridescence, and its fin sliced through the air like a blade. The Survival-nauts, caught off guard, stared in awe and trepidation as the Alpha glided past them, its eyes locking onto theirs with an eerie intelligence. Without a glance at Jack, the Alpha vanished into the dense foliage, leaving behind only the lingering sense of its formidable presence.

The Survival-nauts, hearts pounding, exchanged puzzled glances. The encounter with the alien shark hybrid had been brief, yet it left a question in their head. "Why make itself known?" Jack asked aloud, "What does it hope to gain by scaring us?" Mikhael stopped him. "It's letting us know that it's hunting us, too." Alex spoke up, "No, it's most likely just warning us. Look, we're so far from where it killed Hosiah. There's no reason for it to attack us here." Milo and Meelo agreed, "Yeah, we're out of its territory." The group silently searched for a clearing to make a camp for the night; only being a few hours' hike from their destination, their travels seemed too soon be over. As Jack closed his eyes, he felt a strange vibration and the humming began. Soon after there was a loud crack in the sky as green hues lit up the sky once more. This time, the light did not go away after five seconds. The light continued to burn until sunrise, all the while Jack was exploring an unknown world...

4

Dream walking, with friends!

For every time the light appeared in the sky, Jack would find something new. A large tower, a voice in the distance. Each looming with a threat of death beneath their façade. The light brightly lit the sky over Delta Psi, shining over the faces of the survival-nauts as they slept. Jack's heart began pounding as the wails of his neighbors and his friends could be heard, as usual, he awoke in a strange part of the city. The pyramids just happened to be a new instance, intertwined with his dreamscape. Mikhael reached out and grabbed his arm, "Is this... Real? I've said I wanted to see heaven, Jack, but I never imagined this. This is the worst thing imaginable." Jack turned to see his other friends, standing nearby one another in similar positions to how they slept. "Are you all okay?" Jack quickly began feeling each of them, ensuring they were in fact, real. "How... How are you here?" He stepped back and looked over each of them. Meelo reached out for Milo and the two held each other tight. "I've got you, sister." He spoke softly as he embraced her. "We'll get out of this, just you wait. I'm sure that Jack has it all figured out." In truth, Jack was just as confused as they were. His mind was racing with questions, *how are they here? Why are they here?* His thoughts came to an abrupt halt as the voice called out to him once more. "Bring us the key, Jack. Let us restore humanity."

"Restore humanity?" Mikhael questioned the voice. "We here on Delta Psi are all that is left of humanity. We left Earth, years ago!" Jack whipped his head around, surprised that his friend could hear the voice. "Yeah!" Sarah rose her fist, "We don't have to restore it, we're still here!" A loud humming fell over their dreamworld, droning out even the sounds of the screams from before. One moment, Sarah was standing with the group. The next, she was flung through the air as if lifted by an entity much larger than she. The voice rang out through the droning, "YOU WILL LISTEN OR YOU WILL BE FORGOTTEN!" A dark shroud fell over Sarah and the green hue filled it. After a few seconds, the light was gone and so was Sarah. "WE WILL ENSURE DELETION OF THOSE WHO OPPOSE." The others quickly attempted to run and found themselves running in the air, unmoving from their positions. "What do you hope to achieve?" Jack asked with a sense of worry in his voice. "We're only kids!" Alex shouted, unable to contain himself any longer. "So, you're only option is to kill us if you can't save us?" Jack questioned the voice as the hum continued. "Some saviors you are." The droning slowly faded as the voice returned, softly. "That is why we need you, the key..." Jack struggled to turn himself around as he floated in place, "Well, Mikhael. What do you suggest we do?" Bart chimed in, breaking his silence. "I say we do what they say, we give them Jack." Mikhael shook his head and as soon as his lips moved a silence fell on everyone's ears. Jack watched as Mikhael's lips moved but no words could be heard. His movements slowed and the green hue filled the sky, ending their team dream walk. As they opened their eyes, the screams continued. As the light flared across the sky, one of their classmates could be heard screaming from down the hill. Afraid of what they might find, the survival-nauts quickly packed their things and made their way to the rendezvous point, leaving Sarah's body behind. "We're only an hour hike from here!" Alex shouted as he took off in a full sprint down the mountain side. "We should hurry to the rendezvous!" The others quickly followed, stumbling over rocks and tree branches as they traversed the mountain. "The cabin should be just up there in the clearing." Jack pointed to a hill across the small valley from them as a strange ship broke through the atmosphere and came barreling towards the rendezvous point. "Now, I bet that's Krollo!" Jack shouted as he pointed out the ship. Its strange look resembling a fish as it dashed across the sky.

The light streams following behind it, like the light that had been terrorizing the people of Delta Psi for the last few days. "We've got to make it to the rendezvous!" Jack pressed on, pulling his friends with him. As they neared a steep cliff and a waterfall, they all looked for a different way down the mountain than using the cliff, to no avail. Milo searched along the cliff for a way down and found a place where previous participants in the survival test had climbed down using vines. "Come on, I found a way down!" He shouted as he began to climb down the vines. The others quickly joined him and watched as he climbed down the forty-foot cliff. After what seemed like forever, Milo reached the bottom, safely placing his feet on the ground. The survival-nauts all cheered as they readied his sister, Meelo, to descend the cliff. Another 30 minutes passed by the time she reached the bottom. Next was Alex, quickly sliding down the vine without wasting any time. Bart shrugged his shoulders as he glanced at Mikhael and Jack who were still watching Alex and began his descent. As Bart reached the halfway point in the vine, he heard a rattling noise, like the sound his grandmother's rain maker used to make. An object from the old days, it had no use on Delta Psi besides a novelty. He looked above him, directly at what had made the noise. A snake, a rattlesnake, no less. His fingers gripped tightly as he began to panic, "I don't want to get bitten!" Being twenty feet off the ground held its consequences when dealing with a snake, such as the inability to hold on to something like a ledge or a vine. Bart's grip slipped loose of the vine and his foot fell from the ledge as he fell backwards off the vine the remaining twenty feet. The others quickly flocked to him as he gasped for air, a drop of blood slowly fell from his nose as they picked him up. "Is he okay?" Mikhael yelled to them, "He's got the wind knocked out of him, but he's okay!" Alex shouted back. Jack slapped Mikhael on the arm, "Well, now how are we going to get down? The only path has a snake in it." Mikhael looked around at the foliage growing around them, "Why not just make another rope out of the vines and make our own path?" Mikhael pointed to the large group of vines hanging from a tree. "Those look like they'll do just fine."

The boys quickly began fashioning another rope from the vines, wasting no time as they bound them together. Their hearts pounding as they felt themselves coming ever closer to their destination. Jack threw the vines over the cliff after tying one end to one of the larger trees, "Now, who's up first?" Jack asked as he looked over the edge. Mikhael slapped him on the shoulder, "You, old pal. You tied them together; you should be the one to test them!" He grinned wide, showing his teeth. "No offense!" Jack quickly locked eyes with Mikhael and peered over the ledge, "Okay, I guess I'll go first." He began his descent, weary at first and soon realized the vines were safe. Jack quickly shuffled down the vines and placed his feet on the ground. "Okay, Mikhael. It's your turn!" He shouted from the bottom. Mikhael peered over with a look of disgust on his face. "Are you sure?" he asked as he threw his leg over the ledge and began to climb down. "I don't want to fall because you lied to me, Jack." Jack shouted back, "It's fine, I promise!" Their shouting echoing off the canyon could have been heard by anyone in the area, to their luck, the alpha happened to hear them. It quickly made its way through the brush and down the river, following their shouts. As Mikhael made it halfway down the vine, the alpha popped its head over the ledge. Its eyes, fierce and hungry, it searched for a way to get the boy closest to it. Swiping its claws down the cliff at him, it noticed the vines he was hanging from were running to a tree behind him. Jack and the others were all motioning and shouting at Mikhael to hurry up, afraid the alpha may jump down and attack them. Mikhael began to shuffle a little faster, trying not to slip as he shuffled when he felt a tug on the vine. Another tug, and soon he was being pulled back up the cliff. "Help!" He shouted as he tried to shuffle down the vine. Jack quickly grabbed the end of the vine and began to pull it downward, "Help me!" He shouted to the others who quickly joined him in his game of Tuggle war. They all pulled with all their might as Mikhael got closer to them; just as he was ten feet from them, the vine came loose, and he came toppling down onto his friends. They all shouted in hoorah that nobody was hurt as they helped Mikhael to his feet and began running towards the rendezvous, their hearts pounding with the anticipation of completing their test. Alex noticed a few of the other students running across the field, parallel to them. As they made their way across, another of the hybrids came out from the bushes and attacked them. Their death, imminent as the strange aliens grew closer. The survival-nauts ran all the way past the fish-like ship and burst the door open. Jack was the first to enter, his mind at ease as he seen the familiar face turn around. "Alone, you are not, Jack. Dream walking you have done?" The alien pointed to the other survival-nauts, "Yes, together you have. Go we must, the life here dead. The Zakarah move on land, water. They kill all things not them, eat them." Jack and the others all looked around at one another, "The Zakarah?" Jack asked, "You mean, the shark thing that killed our friends?" Mikhael spoke up, "And almost killed me!"

Krollo gazed at the panic-stricken faces of the children, "With Jack, we have key. We go to Attagascia. No panic, children." He raised his arms as if to show he came in peace. "I help!" He reached down to his belt and pulled off something that resembled a tentacle and whipped it like it was a knife and it let loose a blast through the window of the cabin, killing one of the Zakarah. "We go, in ship." He motioned to his ship as the hatch lowered in the back. "We go to home, my home." The children all began to worry about their parents and their other friends, "So, everyone else is just... Dead?" Bart asked, "And we're supposed to just go with you and accept that?" Jack turned to him and began to explain, "I'm sorry. Bart. I know this is all a little crazy, but I've been here before. We should go with him; you don't want to go home. What you'll find there is not what you'd ever want to see." Bart gave Jack a look over, "And how am I supposed to trust you? I think I'll take my chances with Mr. Clark coming to get me. He should be here soon." The others quickly began to try to change his mind, but he turned and ran to the room in the cabin and shut the door. "It no big deal, he come back." Krollo began to board his ship, "Now, come. We go." He motioned for the children to follow. Jack was first, followed by Mikhael and soon after the others, one by one except for the twins who ran together. The ship began to power up as Jack turned to look back at the cabin, surrounded by Zakarah and other students attempting to fight them off as they flew away. The walls of the ship were sleek and slimy, wet, just like Krollo. Jack ran his fingers along the wall as he joined the others in the cargo area. As the kids all looked amongst one another, the strange light shown in the sky, this time the children were able to watch what happened below them. The Zakarah all began shooting rays of light from their eyes, along with the kids at the cabin, and they all fell still. A silence fell over Delta Psi as they slowly left the great stone mountains. Jack weaved his way through the others to make his way to the cockpit, in hopes of some explanation from Krollo. As he opened the doorway, a light fell over his eyes and he fell back, flat on his back. His eyes lit green as he drifted off into sleep. Mikhael rushed over to help but he was soon overtaken with the same dilemma and collapsed right next to him. The others took no time joining them as their ship quickly made it into space and began its warp jump, causing their limp bodies to float about in the cargo bay as they began to dream. Krollo set the controls to auto-pilot and left his seat, passing the mirror on his way and showing a reflection of Jack, walking briskly by. He made his way through the hall, stopping at the cryo pods only to prepare them for his sleep. Their trip was going to take a few light years, and Krollo didn't want the children to die in the process. He prepared each of the pods and brought the children back to them, their floating bodies much easier to carry than if there had been gravity. As he placed Jack in his cryo-pod, he investigated the boy's face. "You are key. You save system." He whispered as he placed him carefully in the pod. "Yes, key." He grinned as the pod shut and held up the strange object Jack had in his backpack. He walked over and set it on the shelf and shuffled back over to his own cryo pod. "Sleep now, yes." He mumbled as he climbed into the pod. "Tired I am." He closed his eyes as the pod shut. The beeping began for the system to deep freeze for their sleep and Krollo couldn't help but feel something strange. He opened his eyes, and the strange object was glowing green, much like the light. "No!" He shouted as the freeze began, flash freezing him in position, along with the survival-nauts.

To be continued...

As a reader, you are *very* **special**. Your point in this world is to keep the **story,** alive!

So, I'd like to say Thank you.

As I pen down these words, my heart swells with gratitude for each one of you who embarked on the journey within the pages of my book. It's a profound honor to have you as companions on this literary adventure.

Writing is a solitary endeavor, but your presence transforms it into a shared experience, a vibrant tapestry woven with the threads of your imagination and mine. Your decision to invest your time and thoughts in the world I've created is a gift beyond measure.

Thank you for allowing my words to dance in your mind, for breathing life into characters and places born from the recesses of my imagination. Your readership is the heartbeat that resonates through the pages, turning mere words into a symphony of emotions.

Every reader is a beacon of light, illuminating the path of an author's journey. Your curiosity, your empathy, and your willingness to explore the realms of fiction make this endeavor worthwhile. It's not just a book; it's a connection forged between us, transcending time and space.

I'm genuinely grateful for the support, the encouragement, and the conversations that have blossomed around this book. Your feedback, whether it's a kind word or constructive critique, is the nourishment that helps an author grow.

In a world bustling with myriad distractions, your choice to spend time in the world I've created is a cherished gift. It's my hope that my words have resonated with you, sparked your imagination, or maybe offered a moment of respite from the complexities of life.

As you close the cover and reflect on the journey we've shared, know that you've left an indelible mark on the story. Thank you for being a vital part of this narrative, and may the echoes of our shared adventure linger in your heart. Welcome to the Odyssey.

With deepest gratitude,

Jerry T. Cook

Jerry T. Cook

"Life has taken a toll on some, and for some, it's taken their life."

Jerry began his journey as a writer in the year 1998 when he was first called "Storytelling Jerry".
After working in the labor industry as a well technician beginning at the age of sixteen, Jerry learned about geography and water quality including many other technical skills required to bring water to the top of the ground.
Through the years; Jerry's physical health had worsened since he was born with a birth defect and he decided to try another route in his life path: becoming a millwright.
After working as a millwright for 2 years, Jerry took the exam and became a Journeyman. At this point in his life it became too difficult for him to perform the tasks of his career and then he had to stop working.
As a stay-at-home dad, Jerry now writes beautiful works of fiction for everyone to enjoy.

If you're interested in reading more work by Jerry T. Cook

Please check out his website at

Https://storytellingjerrysbooks.mailchimpsites.com

The Structure-Word Search

```
H A M F Q A T T A G A S C I A H B C D G
U J E M U C R K D I G T J E E U R A M I
O N V L R K Q H T N Z Y A S M I L G Y F
T L I G H T E B B E G Q C G G K C D Z C
X W O S M U K Y P M P C K S F A O K D F
K F N N Q N K H U E O F A V U L M F U V
H T E J Y M L R R E K B W I I C U K O V
Q I H Y U R C F I L Q A Q O O H A W D O
V L B L H I F U B O S R Y Y L P J Y U W
H H R V O J E S S E Z T Q N V G J W Y S
Z R Z R M A L D R E A M W A L K E R G I
I L S U C Q Q R E P S P I I A R M U Z O
M G U F X P I F J L V K T T G K I W Z U
S F R C Q X F N A D T W J D Z M L B W X
T H V H F U X K L Q M A I U M I O H E A
L N I B G S B X E B L P P P M K I C W J
B F V R P X C F X M V Y Z S D H A Q W P
A A A P L A J Y W D O U Z F I A Y D F P
W S L E Y R S A R A H X Y K H E C Y Z G
N X A Q E A V G B E G A F V D L Z O K F
```

Dream walker	Attagascia	Delta Psi	Jack
Mikhael	Survival	Sarah	Bart
Jesse	Meelo	Light	Milo
Alex